THE

OLD

HOUSE

To my family and friends with love, to Sisters of the Blessed Sacrament With Love.

TERESA CAHILL

THE

OLD

HOUSE

First published in 2017 by
Teresa Cahill
Dublin
Ireland

Paperback	ISBN: 978-1-78846-000-2
eBook – mobi format	ISBN: 978-1-78846-001-9
eBook – ePub format	ISBN: 978-1-78846-002-6
CreateSpace paperback	ISBN: 978-1-78846-003-3

Produced by Kazoo Independent Publishing Services
222 Beech Park, Lucan, Co. Dublin
www.kazoopublishing.com

Kazoo Independent Publishing Services is not the publisher of this work. All rights and responsibilities pertaining to this work remain with Teresa Cahill.

Kazoo offers independent authors a full range of publishing services. For further details visit www.kazoopublishing.com

Cover design by Andrew Brown
Printed in the EU

ACKNOWLEDGEMENT

Sisters of the Blessed Sacrament, Cahill Family, Friends. Chenile Keogh, Robert Doran and Kazoo Independent Publishing Service. To all who read this book.

CHAPTER ONE

———◇———

NORA CROKE JOGGED PAST THE dilapidated old house every day. She had felt drawn to it since she moved back to Latimore four years ago and often wondered about its owners and past, its memories and history. Its uncared-for state and wild appearance with its overgrown landscape appealed greatly to Nora. She loved to have things neat and tidy, and her dream was to return the house to its original appearance.

The fields surrounding it gave it a rugged look. A little beyond the gateway there was a large, old, gnarled oak tree. During the spring and summer it was inhabited by birds of all kinds. People were able to walk around the grounds, as the gates had a side opening which led into the grounds. The children of Latimore played on the lower branches of this 400-year-old tree. The tree had a history, and Nora had heard the legend. According to the townspeople, if a branch of the tree broke off, the owners would lose a member of the family. This myth had been talked about for years but with no real evidence to back it up.

The land was enclosed by a high wall, and the turrets of the house could be seen from the main road. In summertime, families often had picnics there and walked down to the low-lying cave near the border wall. It was their favourite haunt. In the springtime, bluebells and whitebells appeared in the wildness of the surrounding wood. Daffodils, dressed in yellow, added colour to the landscape. Long, winding paths led through the wood to the house. In the summer, they were covered by the trees' green leafy splendour. Even in the bright sunshine it could be very dark, but its peace and tranquillity gave it an otherworldly appearance.

One morning as she passed, Nora thought she saw a child playing near the gate. Unsure if this was the case, she doubled back to check, but no one was there. Nora shook herself and blamed her imagination.

In the spring, four years ago, Nora had being diagnosed with cancer. It had been a very traumatic time for her. Her mother was ill at the same time and also in hospital. When the doctor told her he was going to operate on her she went into shock and was stunned. All she could do was let the doctor do his work and hope she would be alive at the end of the ordeal. When her family came to visit, she told them that the operation had gone well.

'Thank God that it is over. I was terribly afraid and worried that I could not take care of Mam. I know you were there for me,' she told them.

'Get well and don't worry, as we'll continue to care for you both,' her brother Rick assured her.

Nora told the family that after leaving hospital she would have her chemotherapy first, and then she would build herself up. She informed them of her other plans, which were to publish her writings. After her stay in hospital, she went home to Latimore and took care of herself. It was difficult to work, so she took time off. She struggled with depression, but her writing, family and friends helped her find a way out of it.

She had travelled to France and England when she was younger but now planned to settle down in Latimore. She found a part-time job with a firm of solicitors, Hanks and Co. She recalled her first day on this new job and meeting Anita Walsh. She was very apprehensive, as it was a job she had never done before. After a while she began to settle down. The job gave her time to do things she wanted to: going for walks, attending writing and book clubs, usually in the evenings, and meeting up with her friends for lunch or coffee. Life was very good for Nora.

One morning, after her usual walk, she put on her navy suit and settled down to breakfast before going out to work. Suddenly her doorbell chimed. She wondered who it was at that time in the morning and went to answer the door. Tom Lynch, the postman, handed her a bundle of letters which she presumed were all bills.

'Nora, I have a registered letter for you. Would you sign for it, please?' Tom asked, handing her the form and disturbing her thoughts.

A letter from her mother drew her attention, and she opened it. Immediately she realised her life would change forever. She read the letter over and over again and could not believe her eyes. Her mother wanted her to come home to Kilkenny because she had received a letter from a firm of solicitors who were dealing with her uncle's estate. Her mother wrote that she was worried about the letter. Nora was well aware that her mother tended to worry when it was not necessary, but she set off home nonetheless.

'Mam, I'm home!' she called.

'I am in the attic!' her mother, Elizabeth, replied.

'What are you doing up there?'

'Looking for diaries your father wrote,' Elizabeth replied. 'Can you put the kettle on, please?'

Nora plugged in the kettle and put mugs on the table. Her mother came down with five diaries in her arms and put them on the table.

'I could not find the sixth diary,' she said, gasping for breath.

Nora poured her a mug of tea, and her mother handed her the letter. It was from a firm of solicitors, Malay & Malay, from Knightsbridge in London. Nora read it quickly.

Dear Ms Croke,

We offer you our sympathy on the death of your uncle, Richard Croke. You are the chief beneficiary of his will along with your family. We have arranged for some immediate details to be sent to a firm of solicitors in Kilkenny. Their address is attached. Could you contact them as soon as possible? Further documentation is currently being prepared by your uncle's Irish solicitors in Latimore.

Yours sincerely,
Tom Malay

'But this is addressed to me,' Nora said. She looked at the envelope. It was her mother's address, but it had her name on it. Nora thought this odd. 'What has this to do with the diaries?' she asked her mother.

'Your dad always told me he had written the diaries, six of them, but not to read them until after his death,' Elizabeth Croke said. 'Your uncle Richard was your father's brother, not mine.'

Nora knew the diaries had always puzzled her mother, so she was surprised to see her handing them to her.

'You have them and read them. I prefer to let things be. Be careful of your own brother, Billy, as he has always had a desire to possess them,' Elizabeth said.

'OK,' Nora said, putting them away. 'You said there were six. Where is the last one?'

'Follow me,' said Elizabeth, leading her into her bedroom. She remembered there was one hidden in a box in a secret space under her shoe rack in the wardrobe. Elizabeth pulled out a small black leather case which had the words 'Diary No. 6' written on it. Nora put it along with the others in her own bedroom. As she was coming out, the doorbell chimed.

'That is your brother, Billy. He comes every day,' her mother said.

Nora opened the door and started to greet him, but he demanded to know why she had suddenly come home. For her mother's sake, Nora refrained from being cross.

Billy lived in an apartment on the quays in Dublin. He was thirty years old, divorced and ill-tempered. As a sales representative for a pharmaceutical company, he travelled a great deal up and down the country and was often abroad. Nora was well aware that her brother was a bully who cared only for himself. As such, he had few friends and no close relationships with women. He was handsome, with black hair and a goatee, but Nora had no doubt that despite his excellent physical health, Billy had mental health issues that manifested in his bad temper.

Both brother and sister went their own way after the death of their father.

'Just on a day visit,' she lied. 'Mam and I are going shopping for a few hours.'

Elizabeth said nothing and decided to play along. She got herself ready while the two siblings sat lost in their own thoughts. Nora went upstairs, put the diaries into her large bag and headed out to her car.

'We'll see you later,' she said, leaving her brother stunned but with a smirk on his face.

As Nora drove, Elizabeth explained that Billy had wanted to read the diaries for a long time, but she just did not trust him.

'He knows about them?' Nora asked.

'Yes. Your father always said he was not to read them until he had died,' Elizabeth replied. 'He will search for them while we are out.'

'Well, he won't because he is following us!' Nora said.

Nora turned her car and headed up a side street where there was a little shop. Her brother missed the turn and got delayed, giving Nora time to park, grab her bag and walk to the solicitors with her mother.

'Miss Croke and Mrs Croke, welcome, come in and please be seated,' said a senior solicitor who then explained to Elizabeth about the letter sent to her but addressed to Nora. He also revealed that her uncle's solicitors in Latimore was Hanks and Co. Nora couldn't believe the strange coincidence.

There was a knock on the door and Billy burst in. 'Thought you would leave me out?' he said.

'No! We did not know you were invited,' Nora said, before introducing her brother to the solicitor.

'Well, young man, you were not invited, as this part of the will does not concern you,' the solicitor replied.

'What will?' Billy stammered. 'I am asking for the diaries.' He left quickly without another word.

Elizabeth was worried, as she knew her son's temper. The solicitor gave the letter to Nora to read. She showed the letter to her mother.

Stunned and excited they both left and returned home. On arriving they found the house ransacked, and after calling the Gardaí realised who had done it. Billy had disappeared. They explained to the Gardaí what had happened, and that they were sure Billy had done it. When the Gardaí left to start their investigations, Nora and her mother were upset about the house but after Nora's good luck they did not let it dampen their spirits. Nora had a lot of questions to ask but she decided to wait.

'What about the diaries?' she asked her mother.

'You take them and read them but not here, as Billy may return.'

The next day Nora was so excited and could barely contain herself. She couldn't wait to get to work and show the letter to her friend and colleague, Anita Walsh, who also worked with Hanks and Co. She would not tell her about the diaries though.

Some time ago, Anita Walsh had sat by the river near the wooden bridge at the bottom of her garden. A slight breeze fanned her shoulder-length hair off her face as she gazed at the silver water twisting into a whirlpool. She was deep in thought. The swirling water matched her troubled thoughts about the loss of her job and her search for a new one, which was proving difficult in this recession. While she gazed at the water curling down into a narrow tail and twisting up again into a wider space, she recalled her father's wisdom and missed his presence. Anita shook herself and went home.

As she opened her door, the warmth of the cottage greeted her. While waiting for the kettle to boil she rummaged in the messy kitchen drawer for a biro or pencil but none could be found. Instead, she came across a poem in her grandmother's handwriting. She read and reread the line, 'When all is gone, look at what is left, move on'. Anita asked herself what she had left to do. It was then she realised the importance of her hobby of painting. She went out to her father's shed to recover some of her brushes and found one of the tools he had used for sculpture. She recalled playing with some of them as a child. When she returned to the kitchen with her brushes and sculpture tools, excitement ran through her veins as she felt the thrill of something new. But she needed a part-time job to help her start up a new business. The spare room would suit her venture well, so she decided to set it up as a workshop. With a cup of tea beside her, she sketched the whirlpool. Satisfied with the drawing, she started to paint it. Then she found a piece of wood and sculptured it into a fruit bowl.

A short time later, Anita had an interview for a new job as a secretary in Hanks and Co. With time to spare, she went to the café and ordered a cappuccino. Sitting in an alcove window space, she looked out onto the car park. Her attention was drawn to a man ordering a coffee. As the café was full, the man asked to sit down at her table.

'I am Tom Hanks,' he said, introducing himself.

'Anita Walsh,' she replied, and sipped her coffee. Her mind was on the forthcoming interview, and she wondered if he was related in any way to the solicitors she was on her way to. A noise distracted her, and when she glanced up she found Tom looking at her. 'Sorry, did you say something?' she asked.

'Yes, I did,' he replied. 'I need help in my office, and I was wondering if you needed a job?

'Yes I do, need a job that is, and I am on the way to an interview for one. It could very well be for the job that you are referring to,' she said. Despite his two-piece Armani suit, Anita thought he looked a bit scruffy to work in an office.

They established that it was indeed the same job, which amused him greatly. He offered her the job, but before she could reply, his phone vibrated. He grabbed it and left to answer it. While he was gone, Anita left for her interview. When she arrived at the solicitor's office, the receptionist informed her that the interview was cancelled. Anita explained what had happened: Mr Hanks had given her the job.

She was shown where her desk was and what the work entailed. Anita worked until one o'clock. On her way home she noticed some commotion near her house. A Garda stopped her as she approached, and Anita explained that her house was just up the road. Mr Hanks, her new boss, saw her and asked what she was doing there. She repeated what she had said to the Garda.

'What has happened?' she asked Mr Hanks.

'A young man has climbed a tree and is sitting on one of the branches which hang over the whirlpool,' he replied, blushing.

'My house is further up and I have climbing ropes in the shed. I will phone the climbing club to come and help,' she told him.

When the young man was safely on the ground and the Gardaí had left the scene, Anita took the ropes and ladder home.

The following day at work, Mr Hanks approached her and thanked her for her assistance during the incident at the whirlpool. When she returned home after work, she found an envelope on the mat. It was an invitation to Mr Hanks' house for the following evening. She phoned to accept and decided she would wear her black dress with its small jacket and the pearl necklace her late husband had given her. Anita began painting for a while and suddenly realised she had put her late husband and a younger man standing on the bridge into the painting.

The next evening Anita arrived at Mr Hanks' door. The most beautiful woman opened it and Anita stared open-mouthed at her. She had not known she was in a wheelchair and apologised for staring.

'Come in and don't apologise. It happens often,' Marie Hanks said, smiling. Anita handed Marie a painting of a beautiful yellow rose bush. Marie was delighted, explaining that she could not have flowers in the house because the pollen affected her lungs.

In the living room, Anita was greeted by Mr Hanks and the young man who had been rescued the day before. He introduced the young man to her. He was his son, Sean. During the evening Anita observed how content everyone seemed.

'What were you doing up the tree?' Anita asked Sean when he sat beside her.

'I wanted to look into the whirlpool without getting too near,' he replied sheepishly.

'Join the climbing club,' she said, handing him the address of the owner.

The following day in the office, Mr Hanks asked Anita to assess the applicants who had replied to the advert for a second secretary.

In them she noticed one who seemed to fit the job description. She prepared the interview for Mr Hanks, and she sent for Nora Croke.

Anita helped Nora settle into both her new job and Latimore. They quickly became firm friends, so it was natural for Nora to share her good news with her colleague when she arrived at work following her eventful trip to her mother's in Kilkenny.

'Wow! Congratulations and my sympathy,' Anita said to Nora after reading the letter. Nora asked her when she could speak with Mr Hanks to discuss the letter. Anita cleared his diary for an hour that afternoon for her.

After the initial welcome, Nora handed the letter to Mr Hanks. She marvelled at the coincidence that her uncle had been his client. He asked Anita to bring in the file on Mr Richard Croke, Nora's uncle. Mr Hanks explained that her uncle had lived in Latimore and had bought a large house. He had refurbished some of it and then, because he needed money to pay off some gambling debts, he had left for England. Nora was shocked to find out she had inherited a large house and one million pounds sterling.

'So I am a millionaire!' Nora stammered.

'Yes, you sure are. Well done and congratulations,' he replied.

All Nora's family received small gifts. Her uncle had known of Nora's love for the house and wanted her to have it. When she received the address of her inheritance, she realised that it was the old house she looked at each morning.

'I did not realise he lived in Latimore. I never met him,' said Nora.

'Even though your uncle kept to himself, he was interested in everything. He kept in touch with me over the years about your family. I also told him that you worked for me now, and he was very pleased. Unfortunately he had a heart condition so he knew that time for him was limited,' Mr Hanks replied.

Nora was stunned and had one more question. 'Why did my uncle move away?'

Mr Hanks replied, 'I may have been his solicitor, but he told me very little. It is my belief that he needed money. He tended to gamble, Nora.'

Nora puzzled over this. She realised his gambling addiction was the reason for his sudden departure. Mr Hanks suggested that Nora take the rest of the day off. Anita would join her when she finished work. She told Anita that she was going for a coffee to the nearest café so that she could absorb everything she had just heard. Then she phoned her brother, Rick.

'Rick, I received a letter from the solicitors in England. Uncle Richard has died and he has left us gifts in his will. I have inherited his house here in Latimore and one million pounds sterling,' she informed him.

'We have all received a letter from the solicitors, and we are delighted about the contents,' he replied. 'Wow! I am pleased you got the house. I saw it once when I was a child. You are now a millionaire. Get out the champagne, and we'll help you celebrate and spend!'

'Well, the house is neglected at the moment and will take a great deal of work and money to return it to its former state,' she told him.

After some chat, she rang her other brother, Billy. When she had congratulated him on his inheritance, she inquired, 'Billy, could you tell me what you know about Uncle Richard?'

'Well, as far as I know he left under a dark cloud, but you can find out for yourself!' he told her sharply, a sign which showed he was angry. 'The old house, it is not too bad, is it?' Billy added regretfully.

'When were you last in it?' she asked him.

'Some years ago,' he replied aggressively because he had just lied.

'Jealousy does not suit you, Billy. But why won't you tell me why he left?' she asked.

'Because I don't know why he left!' Billy replied. 'I wish I had inherited the house and the diaries.'

'What would you do with it?' Nora asked.

'I would knock it down and build flats on the land,' he stated.

'A good job then he gave it to me,' she said and closed her

mobile. It was clear he still wanted the diaries, and Nora decided to read them as soon as possible to see what they contained.

Anita arrived at the café just as Nora hung up on Billy.

'That was my brother, Billy, and he is suffering from jealousy,' Nora informed Anita as she sat down beside her. Nora ordered coffee for them both. While waiting, Nora said, 'I am shocked though excited at having my own house, but when I received the address, keys and the deeds from Mr Hanks, only then did I realise it's the old house I pass each morning. It is in a dreadful state, and now I need to do something about it, especially since I've been complaining about the owners for so long. Good heavens! Now I'm the owner.'

Anita and Nora looked at the deeds of the house which Mr Hanks had put into a large envelope. As the table was small, they finished their coffee before looking over them together.

'I can't take it in that I am a millionaire,' said Nora. 'I lodged the cheque into my bank account on my way here. I appreciate the way my uncle had seen to everything, even paying for my consultation.' Nora shared her hopes and dreams for the house with Anita.

When she returned home, she put on her outdoor leisure clothes. She walked to the old house to view it as the owner. Her stomach was in a tight ball. She could not believe her good luck. As she walked around it, she felt a strong desire to enter, but she felt afraid. She had the feeling that someone else lived there and that someone was watching her. Even though she had the key, she didn't go in. She wondered if the stories of the ghost were having an effect on her. She decided to wait until she could have Anita with her.

Later that evening, relaxing with a glass of wine, she went through the deeds again. She discovered a personal letter addressed to her from her uncle. It was stuck to the back of one of the pages. She hadn't noticed it earlier when she had first examined the deeds. After opening the envelope, she read what her uncle had written:

The Old House

Dear Nora,

As you are reading this letter, you will have been informed of my death and of my will. As you know, the whole family have received gifts, but I wish for you to live in my old house. Mr Hanks will inform you of the necessary details. The cheque is for your own personal use. I kept in touch with Mr Hanks, and over the years I asked about my family, so I am pleased you are working for him now.

Thank you for accepting the house and taking care of it.

Your loving uncle,
Richard.

Uncle Richard had worked on building sites and eventually owned a building company of his own. He sold it when he retired, keeping his savings for his nieces and nephews.

Excited that all her dreams for the house could now be fulfilled, Nora could not wait to put them into action. When she met Anita the next day at work, she asked if she would help her with redesigning the old house.

'Of course I will,' said Anita excitedly. 'Maybe this evening we can look at the plans and write out what it is exactly you want for the house.'

As the next day was Saturday they planned to view the house. The morning dawned bright, and the weather was warm. Nora was up early and waited for Anita to arrive. She had the rest of the day to start looking at the house. She put a notebook and pen into her bag and was now ready.

Anita arrived on her old bike. Her hands were covered in oil, as her bike chain had caused trouble again. Nora had planned on inviting Anita in for a coffee before heading to the house, but Anita declined as she was too excited about the visit.

'No, I'll just wash my hands, then we can go, as I am dying to see the house,' said Anita.

The Old House

They set off towards the old house. Anita realised that the inheritance of the money had not sunk in with Nora yet, and that the old house was now the only thing important to her.

'How does it feel to be a millionaire?' Anita asked.

'Well, I don't feel different, except that I am so excited to do up this old house and have money to do it. It was a dream up to now,' said Nora.

When they arrived, Nora paused for a moment. 'I am your new owner now,' said Nora, addressing the old house quietly.

With trepidation, she opened the gate. The avenue leading up to the old house was lined with oak trees. It was a lovely sight. They walked on and came to a clearing which offered a view of the fields beside the house. They seemed to have walked into another world. Moving on, they arrived at the front of the house, which had two doors made of oak. The sash windows could be opened from the top or pushed up from the bottom. It was a two-storey house and also contained an attic. On the front, the plaster was pebble-dashed and whitewashed. Beside the entrance was a circle of flowers, evidence of past landscaping.

'Let's go inside and see what surprises are waiting,' said Anita.

Nora opened the doors. They both stepped inside and waited so they could adjust to the light. Immediately, Nora felt a presence but could not see anything, so she let it go. As she had Anita with her, it did not feel too bad. They could now see a large staircase straight in front of them; at first sight, it was beautiful. They decided to visit what looked like rooms on either side of the staircase. They counted four doors and a corridor which led around the staircase.

Nora opened the first door. It was a sitting room. There was furniture in it covered with dust sheets. When they lifted one of the sheets, they discovered a soft black leather suite of furniture with footstools. Nora pulled back the long heavy draped curtains. She saw a lovely view which overlooked the lawn and what was once a garden. Closing the curtains they moved to the next room. When they opened this door, they were both completely shocked. It was a library.

'Wow!' both said in unison as they stared open-mouthed.

When they opened the curtains, they discovered that the whole room was lined from wall to wall with shelves of books. Some were rare, others more modern. Nora recognised some of the authors: Geraldine O'Neill, Canon Sheehan, Ruth Rendell and Eileen Casey. Moving around the room, she came across other well-known authors, including Patricia Cornwall, Colm Keegan, Kieran Carty, Dermot Bolger, David Kitchen, Sarah Webb and many others.

'All my family are avid readers. When they see this they will be astonished,' said Nora, full of awe. 'When they come to visit this is where they will stay. I will not be able to get them to go home!' Nora got increasingly excited, wondering how she would be able to tear herself away from her new library, even to go to work.

Anita brought her down to earth. 'We should carry on into the next room as there seems to be a lot to take in.'

Entering the next room, they found a living room. The fourth room turned out to be a kitchen, which was fully furnished and surprisingly modern. They noticed the room at the back of the staircase. This was a small utility room which also led out into the kitchen garden. Closing all the doors, they moved back into the hallway.

'I won't have much to do except cleaning,' Nora said. She was in total shock and excited at the same time.

Anita invited her to the local hotel for lunch, as it was a while since they had eaten. They left the old house. When they arrived at the hotel, they ordered soup and a roll. While waiting for the order to arrive, they discussed design options. They decided to head back to Nora's apartment after lunch and talk about the plans for the first floor of the house, what they had seen and form some ideas of what could be done.

At her apartment, Nora took out her book and pen, starting with where her uncle had stopped refurbishments of the house and garden. They would then look at the land surrounding the house and where it ended. Nora thought about her uncle and wondered what his connection to the house was and who the previous owners had been. Anita could not answer these questions but suggested that a good place to start would be the library in town. Anita decided to call it a day and left for home, telling Nora that she would see her at work on Monday.

Nora had time to look at what they had written. She opened her laptop, typed it all out and put it into a folder. She decided to update her diary with all that had happened since the letter arrived that fateful morning. She reflected on the one thing she had not mentioned to Anita: the presence she felt in the house. It was barely perceptible, like a touch of a cobweb on her head or air blown across her face. Whatever it was, it seemed only to be in the old house. For a fleeting moment she remembered the child she thought she had seen that morning near the gate.

Nora arrived at work on Monday and arranged to speak with Mr Hanks. Later in the evening, before closing time, she explained to him about her plans for the old house and mentioned her plans of moving in and selling her apartment. There seemed to be no obstacle in the way so the move was decided.

'Would you like me to put the necessary details in motion, for the sale of your apartment?' Mr Hanks asked. 'You could call to see Alan Ladd, an auctioneer, on your way home.'

Nora thought that was a good suggestion. She also decided to ask for time off to work on her move. Mr Hanks agreed. She called into the auctioneer to arrange the sale of her apartment. Mr Ladd's secretary gave her an appointment for two o'clock the following day.

Later that evening, she went for a coffee with Anita. Nora mentioned that she needed help with the lands around the house that she planned to lease to farmers. Anita offered her help, as she had experience in that area. They both went home and Nora was pleased with herself. She could now start planning.

She arrived at her appointment with Mr Ladd, but had to wait for a short time as there was someone in the office with him. It was a small waiting room with limited seating. When the office door opened, Mr Ladd let a young woman out. Nora had time to observe him. He was about thirty, of slim build with brown eyes and bushy eyebrows. She wondered where she had seen him before.

'How can I help you?' he asked.

'My name is Nora Croke. I have just inherited the old house

on the north road and I want to move in, so now I want to sell my apartment. I am currently working for Mr Hanks, who is also my solicitor and is dealing with my affairs. He will give you all the details you need to know,' she said, rushing her words.

Mr Ladd took down her name and address and arranged to view and photograph her apartment. This done, Nora went home and started her packing. Anita was coming over in the afternoon to accompany her to the old house.

The afternoon was ideal for a visit. She could look at the land before any changes were made. She wanted to see it in its original rugged form. She walked around with Anita and saw a few things which she had not noticed before. A rope with a tyre wheel tied to the end of it was hanging on the tree in the middle of the field, and there was a small gate at the other end of the land. When they walked through the gate they came across a very run-down old building, which on closer inspection was the remnants of a cottage. Turning around to head home, she observed a tree house built into the tree – another puzzle to solve. With her notebook full, she thanked Anita for her help and left for home.

She was exhausted by the time she opened her front door. She had a coffee and put her notes into the laptop. She decided to write her feelings into her diary when a sudden thought hit her. She was strongly attracted to Alan Ladd. She still could not remember where she had seen him before, but she knew she liked him. She decided not to dwell on it for the moment, as she had other things on her mind. She phoned Anita to ask her if she would come around the next day, as Mr Ladd was coming to view the apartment. Anita immediately agreed, assuring her of any help she needed. Nora was grateful for Anita. Her thoughts returned to the handsome, pleasant face of Mr Ladd. Her reaction shocked her. She hadn't been even slightly interested in a man for a long time. Nora had always assumed that love and marriage were for others to fret about; they weren't for her. Feeling a little unsettled, she pushed her feelings aside and continued packing and then called it a day.

A few minutes after Anita landed the next morning, Mr Ladd arrived at the apartment. Nora welcomed him but could not prevent herself from blushing. She showed him around the apartment. He left after taking photos and returned to the office to put the apartment on the market.

Once he had gone, Anita said, 'We have the afternoon free. Do you want to go to the old house and inspect it?'

'Yes, I do,' said Nora.

They both went to lunch and then to the house. They arrived at the gate, and Nora inspected the area around it. There was a bush covering the gate. She lifted the branch and saw a plaque nailed to the wall. She drew Anita's attention to the name written on it: 'The Old House'.

CHAPTER TWO

———◇———

NORA AND ANITA OPENED THE gate and went up the avenue to the door. They turned left and came to the field where Nora noticed an oak tree and a rope ladder hanging from it. Anita found a path, and they decided to follow it. It circled the house and went behind the old cottage. Inspecting the cottage, they found that it needed rebuilding. It had a lovely shaped garden at the rear which had gone wild, and there was a gate covered with wild brambles. When Nora opened it, she saw that it led out onto the main road. She realised it was the entrance gate belonging to the cottage. They continued along the path and came back to the oak tree with the rope. They both noticed that it had a tree house which needed repair. Nora liked it, so she noted it down in her book for the builders to refurbish.

As they drew near the building, Nora felt the presence once again. This time it took on a shape – that of a child – which only she saw. Now she wondered if she had gone mad amidst the recent changes in her life. She was suddenly very frightened.

'What's wrong, Nora?' Anita asked. 'You've suddenly turned very pale and very silent.'

Nora was between two minds whether to say anything or keep quiet. She made up her mind to tell Anita about the presence she had felt. 'I seem to be going mad and seeing things that no one else sees, like a ghost,' Nora replied.

'Well, there is a local rumour that a ghost is supposed to walk around these grounds, but few have seen it. They don't know if it is a child or an adult,' Anita said.

'If that is the case, I can confirm it is a child. I have just seen it, and it is a boy of about three years,' Nora stated.

They went back to the house and sat down in the kitchen. Over a coffee, Nora started to tell Anita how overwhelmed she felt about the letter, seeing the will, receiving the money and the house. She omitted the detail of her growing feelings towards Alan Ladd.

'Anita, am I going mad or is it the stress of all the excitement?' Nora asked.

'Well, you are not going mad, but you are very tired and perhaps you need to stop and rest. Why don't you take an extra week off, go away for a few days and when you return we will look at the plans and the upstairs floor,' said Anita.

Nora decided to take Anita's advice and went to Tipperary for a few days. She enjoyed the path walks through the mountains and by the waterfalls that flowed into fast mountain streams. A large mansion which was open to the public allowed her to walk around its grounds. It was a delightful week, and she returned refreshed and full of ideas for her own garden. During her trip away, Nora realised that her time would be best spent working on the house and grounds. She didn't have time for her day job.

On her return she went to work and asked Mr Hanks to accept her resignation. She explained her desire to concentrate on the house and future plans. He accepted, and she planned to go at the end of the week. Anita was happy for Nora but sad to see her go, as she would now only see Nora in the evenings. Nora worked hard to clear her desk and at the end of the week when she left, it felt as if a burden had been lifted. Nora went to find a new bed to put in her new home. When she had found one, she arranged to have it delivered the next day to the old house. When she finished setting up the bedroom, she decided to concentrate on the first floor.

The following day the removers were booked to come to her flat for the big move, and Anita was also coming to help. The day was very busy, but Nora had everything packed and ready to move to the old house. Anita and Nora set off before the movers, who arrived soon after and placed all the furniture into the front sitting room for the moment. When they left, Anita and Nora set about turning the room into a temporary bedroom.

'I'm worried about sleeping here tonight,' Nora said to Anita. She had mixed emotions of excitement and concern.

'It will be alright,' said Anita, 'and you can phone me whenever you want. Nora, you need to write down your plans for the house and land. You need a housekeeper, a researcher to investigate the history of the house and family, and you need to find a gardener. Also you need to find out who you could lease the land to and open a bank account for the rent. The cottage and the tree house need to be refurbished and the grounds landscaped.'

Anita thought it would be an idea to put adverts in the papers to lease the land. A rough draft of the adverts was drawn up. Anita would show it to Mr Hanks for a quick once-over tomorrow, make any changes and send them to the newspapers. Then all Nora had to do was to wait and see what responses she would get. Later, as Anita got up to go, Nora expressed her gratitude again for her help. They agreed to meet up the following evening after Anita finished work.

Finally alone, Nora tried out her new kitchen and made her supper. After that, she settled down to read. Suddenly she felt the presence again. Not knowing what to do, she decided to be very still and see what would happen. The ghost of the child appeared. Nora was scared but remained motionless. As she waited, the child started to play around the table, then he turned, looked at Nora and left.

The last thought Nora had before sleeping was to find out about this child. Like the rest of the house, it was a mystery. She wondered how she could go about getting information about the little boy. She decided to start with Anita when she came over the next day. What exactly did Anita know?

While unpacking boxes the following day, Nora spoke to her friend. 'Anita, can you tell me what you know about the old house and the previous owners?' she asked.

'Well, there was a family who lived here in the late 1800s. A local historian has written a book about them,' Anita replied. 'The book on the Charles family gives a history of their return from

The Old House

India where they had tea plantations. The owner was very well-to-do, as was his wife in her own right. She came from an affluent family and was also an artist. It seems a lot of her paintings of India and of the grounds of the old house went into private ownership, though some hang on these walls too.'

'What is the title of the book?' Nora asked.

'*The History of the Charles Family* by Hugh O'Brien,' Anita replied. 'When you look through your library, try to find it. I am sure it must be there. Your uncle may have bought it to add to his collection. After the Charles family left, a young couple, Tom and Mary McNamara, bought it. They lived here with their three-year-old son. Apparently, one day, Mary McNamara stood in the middle of the field near her home. People said a screaming sound shattered the morning sky. She turned and ran back to the house, and the next day the couple and their child had vanished. They were never seen again. The whole thing remains a mystery. Eventually the house was sold to your uncle, who, as you know, had to move to England before he could finish the refurbishment.'

Nora decided to tell her friend about the presence of the small boy playing in the kitchen while she had supper. Anita seemed a little taken aback, and they both wondered which of the past residents he could possibly be connected to, if any.

The next day Nora set about giving the ground floor a clean to make it habitable. There were a lot of windows, so Nora counted them on the outside first, as she had decided to employ a window cleaner. When she had done this, she noticed there was an extra window which could only be seen from the outside of the house and not from the inside. That evening, Anita phoned to say she was calling round. Mr Ladd also phoned to say he wanted to come around to discuss her apartment. Nora said that was fine. As Nora waited for them, she noticed the ghost of the child again. She felt less frightened this time, though she was glad that company was on its way.

She welcomed Mr Ladd and Anita, both of whom appeared at the front door at the same time. Nora offered Mr Ladd a tour of the house which he accepted with delight. He had always wanted to see the inside of this property. After they examined the ground floor and the stairs that led up to the second floor, Mr Ladd expressed his disappointment that he didn't have time to view upstairs. He had another appointment to attend, but they arranged to meet again on Saturday. Before leaving, Mr Ladd suggested that returning the house to its original form would add greatly to the design of the house.

Nora and Anita decided a visit to the cinema was in order. They could relax before tackling the next step. So they set off for an evening out. Friday was Anita's day off, so she arranged to meet Nora and go over plans for employing people for the house and garden. The lease for the farmers was dealt with, so the grounds near the house and the cottage were next on the list. Anita remembered that Mr Ladd also had a building firm and suggested that Nora ask him to quote for the rebuilding work. Nora agreed and blushed ever so slightly. This didn't escape Anita.

'Nora! Why are you blushing?' Anita asked.

Unable to hide her feelings any longer, Nora decided to come clean to Anita. 'I have fallen in love with Alan Ladd!' she said.

'Does he know how you feel?' asked Anita.

'No! I am not sure if it is love, but I feel very attracted to him. I blush every time I see him,' Nora replied.

Anita smiled kindly. 'Well, you'll be blushing again tomorrow when we meet up with him,' she said.

It was around eleven the following morning when Mr Ladd and Anita came to the house to have a look upstairs. After coffee, the first thing they did was re-count the windows because Nora had told them she believed there was one extra on the outside. To solve the mystery they went upstairs to view the top floor. This floor was neglected, and there was debris everywhere.

'Why is this floor not done and yet the ground floor is? This house is full of mysteries and there are a lot of unanswered questions,' said Nora.

'Well, let's take out the plan of the second floor and see if the layout is similar to downstairs,' said Mr Ladd.

Opening the plans of the house, they saw that it was the same.

'So there are four rooms here too,' Anita said.

'Yes,' replied Nora and Mr Ladd in unison.

The first one they looked into was the master bedroom with a bathroom en-suite. It was covered in dust sheets. Lifting one of these, they found a bed with its sheets and duvet still on it, as if someone had left in a hurry and had not returned. Leaving this room they went into the next, which was empty. There was no furniture at all. Then they went into the third room. It was smaller than the others and had only one window. This seemed peculiar to Nora. The fourth room was also empty. After checking out the four rooms, they decided to go for lunch.

'Maybe after lunch we could return to the house together and review the third room with the single window,' Alan Ladd said.

It appeared that he too was intrigued, and this pleased Nora.

'That would be lovely,' replied the two women together.

'Have you the time to spend looking around a dusty, mysterious old house?' Nora asked him.

'Yes, I do. I love a good mystery,' he replied with a smile.

They enjoyed a light lunch at the local hotel, and sat in an alcove discussing the rooms they had seen. Anita, who had been keenly observing Alan and Nora, deliberately went to the dessert counter so they could be alone for a while.

'Anita tells me you have put adverts in the paper for people to help you with the house,' said Mr Ladd.

'Yes, I have,' Nora replied, suddenly shy now that they were alone.

'Well, I have a builder's firm, and I could help you at a discount.'

'I appreciate your offer and I will accept it, thank you very much,' said Nora.

'Also, would you have any objection to calling me Alan?' he asked.

'No, and my name is Nora, thank you,' said Nora, smiling.

Anita arrived back with three ice creams. She saw that Nora was blushing but kept quiet. Before they returned to the house, Alan called his office to check if there were any urgent messages. As there were none, he left his secretary to lock up. They returned to the old house to re-examine the top floor.

Once inside, they placed their coats on the rack and headed up to the top floor. Nora noticed that the little child ghost was at the top of the stairs but then suddenly disappeared. Walking along the corridor they counted the doors. Like the floor below, there were four. They opened the first door, entered the room and Alan pulled back all the curtains. There were two windows there and a third in the bathroom. They continued through the rooms and counted all the windows. By the time they had searched the fourth and final room, they were convinced of their mystery. The room seemed small and only had one window, unlike all the other rooms.

'Well! Here is a mystery,' said Nora.

'Where is the other window?' Anita asked, considering the possibility of a fake window.

'Let's tap the four walls of this room and if it sounds hollow, we have an extra wall,' Alan said.

Nora took one end of the room, and Anita and Alan took the other.

'This small bit here sounds hollow,' Nora suddenly said.

All three decided to tap again on Nora's side, and sure enough it did sound hollow.

Alan suggested that it would be better to get a sledgehammer, which he could arrange for tomorrow. Nora and Anita agreed. As they were about to go down the stairs, Nora noticed that the little ghost was over by the wall outside the room they had just come from. No one else could see him. She turned back and put a pencil mark on the wall where she had seen him and then followed the others.

Anita had to return home as she had an appointment. Alan accepted Nora's offer of a coffee and they continued the conversation that the management of the house.

'What help are you looking for?' he asked.

'Well, I need a researcher as I want the history of the house and the family looked at. I am also hoping to find a landscape gardener and someone to do the housekeeping. The land is already leased to two local farmers through Mr Hanks,' Nora told him.

'Well, you are going to be kept busy,' Alan replied. 'I have to go now, but I would like to see you again. How would you feel about having dinner with me sometime?'

'Yes, I would love that,' she replied.

They arranged a time for Alan to return the following day to investigate the wall, and they said goodbye. Left to herself, Nora felt her face burning. She was blushing yet again. She went into the kitchen for a fresh coffee and to write down everything that had just happened. While doing this she wondered why the little ghost appeared only to her. She then remembered she had not opened the post and set about doing so. There were a few replies from the adverts. The CV's were interesting, so she rang Anita to tell her about them.

'I have a day off tomorrow. I will call over and we will go through them and select a few to interview,' Anita said.

With the evening before her, Nora decided to reflect on what she hoped could be the beginning of a relationship with Alan Ladd. Delight filled her heart at the thought of having dinner with him. A good night's sleep was what she needed after such a busy day.

Anita arrived early the following morning to select people for interviews. Alan was due later to knock down the wall. Anita noticed Nora was very flushed and asked what was wrong.

'Nothing much,' said Nora. 'Let's have coffee while we discuss the interviews. Oh, and Alan asked me out for dinner.'

Anita was delighted for Nora. When the preparations for the interviews were complete, they waited for Alan to arrive with the hammer. With an hour to spare before his arrival, the two women decided to go to the hotel. Over lunch Anita asked Nora what had happened the previous night.

'Well, Mr Ladd asked me to call him by his Christian name. I discovered I love him, and I am confused!' Nora said.

'Don't fret, Nora. Just see how things go,' Anita replied.

They finished lunch and returned to the house where Alan was waiting for them. He looked like a monster holding the sledgehammer.

Nora laughed. 'You look dangerous with that hammer!'

Upstairs in the room, he tapped on the wall to see where the hollowest part of it was. 'You better stand back as I am going to swing this,' Alan said.

He drove the hammer though the panel of the wall and created a huge hole. He enlarged it, and Nora used the torch they had brought with them. There appeared to be another room behind the wall, but it was too dark to see it properly. As it was Nora's house, it was decided that she should be the one to climb into the large hole and check out the hidden room. Once inside, Nora noticed coolness, almost like a sharp draught. The room was pitch black and seemed small. With the help of her torch, she took some steps forward and was stopped in her tracks. Her knees bumped into something. She shone the torch down to see what it was and saw a small bundle of toys on the floor. She realised that she had also bumped into a bed and shone her light on it. Absolute horror and fear struck Nora like a bolt of lightning. Her arms and legs began to tremble, as there on the bed lay a tiny skeleton of a small child. Unknown to herself she was screaming loudly, which made Anita and Alan storm in through the hole to see what was wrong.

When Alan had taken the ladies back downstairs, he called the Gardaí. All three were highly shaken by their discovery. The Gardaí were not long arriving. The detective in charge introduced himself as Tom Chrisom. He and Sergeant Kerr went upstairs to view the scene and looked around the hidden room. They immediately called in the forensic team and went back downstairs to the kitchen.

'Who is the owner of the house?' Detective Chrisom asked.

'I am the present owner,' Nora said.

'Could you let me have a room to use as an incident room?' he asked.

Nora agreed and answered a few more questions while Anita went about making another pot of tea. The forensic team arrived with their cases, fingerprinting kit and cameras. Before climbing the stairs, they put on their paper jumpsuits, shoe covers and latex gloves. They photographed the outside and inside room and dusted the room for fingerprints.

When the Gardaí had set up their equipment, they went to the top floor where the skeleton was laid out. The pathologist arrived and began to examine the remains. Nora overheard him make a tentative suggestion to Detective Chrisom that the child may have been smothered but that the post-mortem would confirm the cause of death. He arranged to have the little corpse removed before leaving. The rest of the team continued with their work.

Detective Chrisom came back down into the kitchen with Sergeant Kerr to take their statements, starting with Nora. She explained her ownership of the house and why Anita and Alan were with her. She decided to tell them about the ghost child appearing to her. Sightings of ghosts were well known by the locals, but very few had seen the child. Many wondered why there was a ghost associated with the house at all. Alan and Anita gave their statements also. They too knew about the ghost stories.

Detective Chrisom informed them that the top floor was a crime scene so it could not be used. Anita offered Nora a room with her until the Gardaí had finished this investigation. Nora declined as she felt she didn't want to impose. Instead, she decided to move into the local hotel.

After being interviewed, Nora packed a case and booked into the hotel. She informed the detective where she would be and asked if he could keep her informed of progress. He agreed and asked who her solicitor was. She told him it was Mr Hanks.

When Nora arrived at the hotel, she unpacked. Both Alan and Anita checked on her before going home. They all decided an early night was best. They had a few hard weeks ahead.

On returning to her room, Nora took out her diary and poured her frustrations into it. She had it all – a new house and plans – and now it had been taken away because of the mysterious corpse. She was in shock. She felt terribly angry and needed to scream but held back because of her surroundings. She didn't want to frighten the life out of the other guests. The bed felt soft, and the warm colours of the room were very calming. It was just what Nora needed now. Why did she have all this happen to her? The cancer was enough, then an inheritance with a mystery and now a skeleton was discovered. She just wanted her life back.

Nora passed a sleepless night. She had questions and wanted answers. She got up and went downstairs for breakfast. The peace of the silence was a balm to her nerves.

Anita arrived for coffee and asked her if she was alright.

'No, I am going mad. I can't stop thinking about the child ghost, and I am looking for answers. I would love to use Alan's hammer on everything!' she said.

'You are in shock and very stressed as we all are, but I think it is the doctor for you this morning,' Anita said and hauled Nora off.

After visiting the doctor, Anita and Nora returned to the hotel armed with a prescription to help Nora sleep and relax. Anita decided it was time to get Nora focused on something different.

Detective Chrisom came to ask her for spare keys so they could get in and out of the house unhindered. She told them where the spare set was and asked when she would be able to return. He told her that the pathologist had finished with the body, and it had been removed, so she could use the ground floor but not the top for at least three weeks.

Nora decided to return to the old house on the following Monday. Anita stated it would be a good idea to send for those who applied for the jobs to come next Friday for interviews. They booked a small room in the hotel for the day. When Friday arrived, Anita, Nora and Alan set up the interview room. The first person was Rita Mahon for the research position. Her CV was impressive. She was around thirty, quite short and stocky. Her long red hair seemed wild and flowed down her back.

'Could you tell us about your research into antique books?' Nora asked.

'I was always interested in antiques, which I learnt from my father,' Rita replied. 'I studied at UDC and started my first job in Blackwell House in Celbridge, Kildare.'

'Where was your last job?' Anita asked.

'In UDC library,' Rita replied. 'I looked after my parents after I finished in Blackwell House. As my parents have passed away, I need to work.'

'Have you any questions, Alan?' Nora asked.

'No, not at the present time,' he replied, and his eyes remained on his notebook.

The next person to arrive that morning was Peggy Price. She had been a hotel manager and was looking for something less strenuous. A housekeeping role would be ideal, she told them. Anita was happy with her and Nora agreed. Again, they said they would let her know.

To their surprise the next interviewee was Detective Chrisom. His CV had stated his name but not his current job. He put them at their ease and said that he was retiring at the end of the month when this investigation in Nora's house was solved. He had studied landscape gardening in his spare time and was anxious to get started in his new career as soon as possible.

When the interviews were over, Anita and Nora joined Alan for a meal and discussed the applicants. They decided on all three interviewees. Nora excused herself so she could phone each candidate to tell them the good news.

Rita Mahon had left the interview with her fingers crossed she would get the job. She went for coffee. Not long later, a buzzing sound distracted her, and she realised it was her phone. The ID caller revealed it was Nora Croke. She answered and was told she had the job of researching the library, plus the history of the owners of the old house. Rita was delighted. She banged the air with glee to the astonishment of the other customers in the café, and then she went home.

The next day, Rita arrived to view the library. She met Alan Ladd just as she was about to ring the bell. He directed her to Nora.

'Come in, Rita,' Nora said from the kitchen where she had coffee mugs on the table. Rita noticed a lot of activity around the upstairs rooms. Longing to satisfy her curiosity, she sat down and accepted a cup of coffee.

Nora explained all the activity upstairs. Then she told Rita that she wanted to learn about the history of the old house, the family who were previous owners and her uncle. Rita seemed enthusiastic about getting started with the materials in the library. Nora told Rita she would be away for the next few days, and she would see her when she returned.

It was Alan who had suggested that she get away for a few days. With the interviewees notified of the results and with permission from the Gardaí, Nora went home to her mother's. She wanted to talk to her family and hoped to find out some information about her uncle Richard. She received a lot of information and photos, some of which she had never seen before. They prompted a desire to start a family photo history.

On Monday morning, Nora returned to the old house. That evening after work Alan phoned her and asked if she would join him for a meal at the hotel. Nora was delighted and accepted the invitation. When they met at the hotel, he was astounded at the beautiful blue evening dress and matching shawl she was wearing. She felt at ease in his company. They spoke about all the events that had happened. He complimented her on her dress sense and how she handled the inheritance and the discovery of the child. As he escorted her home, he asked if he could see her again, and she agreed. He left her at the door of the old house and waited until she went in. Nora felt very happy, as she liked Alan and thought a lot about him. For now, her diary and bed were more enticing after the excitement of the evening.

The next day the Gardaí arrived to continue processing the room. While they were upstairs, Nora went into what was now her library and looked at the books to see if there was anything about the house in them.

Rita Mahon arrived to see the books and to find out about the research into both families. She was going to talk to local people and see if anyone remembered who had lived in the house. She asked Nora if she had any input into this idea. Nora recommended that Rita speak to Anita and get the name of the local historian she had spoken about previously. She also thought that Alan could be of help. Nora phoned Anita to tell her about Rita and asked her out for coffee after work. Anita agreed and invited Nora over to her house.

While they were chatting over coffee, Alan phoned Nora with the news that he had found some papers about a young family who lived in the old house and had left suddenly, never to be heard of again. They had a gardener who also left. It was the same story that Anita had told her. She asked him to bring the papers over to Anita's house, and she told him she would be hanging on to them to show Rita.

After an hour, Alan and Nora left Anita's and went for a walk around the boundary of the old house. He took note of what the builders could do, and while they found the old cottage in bad repair, it could be refurbished and made to look like new. They arrived back at the gate and said their goodbyes. Her phone rang as she entered the house. Detective Chrisom wanted to meet to ask her a few questions. She agreed and told him that Rita Mahon was going to research the family. He asked her if she could let him have any findings as soon as possible. Heading off for bed, Nora decided to keep her date with her diary and finally went to sleep.

CHAPTER THREE

———◇———

WHEN DETECTIVE CHRISOM ARRIVED, THEY gave him the information about the family's disappearance in the newspaper cuttings Alan had found. He borrowed them to help with the investigation. Nora also contacted Rita about the cuttings. Rita decided to see if the original gardener was still alive. He might be in a nursing home by now. She would be in touch with them when she had news of his whereabouts.

Detective Chrisom asked Nora if she would be interested in selling him the cottage, now that he was going to be her gardener. Nora was delighted with the idea of him purchasing the cottage. She agreed to discuss it with her solicitor as soon as possible. She felt lucky at this turn of events. Nora decided on a quiet evening, as she wanted to update her diary. She had just put the kettle on for a coffee when the phone rang. Annoyed at the interruption, she wondered who it was. Her annoyance abated when she realised it was Alan.

'Would you come out for an evening to the theatre?' he asked.

There went her quiet evening in, but company would be a welcome option. She said yes. Preparing herself for the evening out cheered her up. It was *Joseph and the Amazing Technicolour Dreamcoat*, a very enjoyable musical show based on a biblical story. After the show they went for a quiet drink and a chat.

Nora decided to speak to Alan again about her sightings of the child ghost. He knew there was a ghost but had never seen it. Nora felt as if she was going mad and was even considering moving out.

'Don't, at least not yet,' Alan said. 'Wait until the investigation is over and then see if you are of the same mind.'

'Yes, alright,' Nora replied.

They then set off for home, and Alan asked if he could see her the following day. She agreed, he kissed her goodnight and he headed home. Nora opened her doors and leaned against them with a sigh. Her feelings were now totally confused. She was not aware of her ghost friend watching. She decided to write in her diary. This usually helped her sleep and now was no exception.

The day dawned cold, and frost covered the land like a white sheet. In her diary she had written her plans with the intention of carrying them out before the house became invaded once more. The builders arrived and went over the plans for the cottage. She informed them that Detective Chrisom was buying it, and he had his own plans for it. They could start on clearing around it and also the tree house. While the builders continued working on the cottage, the Gardaí arrived to continue their investigations on the top floor.

Nora decided to check out the basement and see what was down there. It was full of rubbish, and she realised a skip was needed to clear it out. She found an old locked trunk and set it aside until Detective Chrisom or Alan came round. She found an old desk full of documents in large envelopes. Nora filled a refuse bag with them and marked it. The rest of the stuff was old junk which did not seem to have any value, so she let it go for the skip. She asked one of the Gardaí if he could try to open the trunk, which he managed to do. Inside, Nora found the most beautiful white wedding dress imaginable, wrapped in fine tissue paper. Nora phoned Anita and told her what she had found.

Anita called over after work and asked her what she would do with the dress.

'I am going to have it cleaned, and then I'm going to put it away safely,' Nora said.

Nora had to change her clothes, as she was covered in dust. When Alan came over, Nora explained about finding the envelopes of documents, but she didn't mention the dress. Everyone else also kept quiet, which Nora was glad of. Detective Chrisom arrived to examine the documents. He took them to a table and told Nora and Alan they could head out, as he would be there for some time. Anita would be there if he needed anything. They could enjoy themselves.

Nora and Alan went for a meal, as he had something to tell her. He explained that he had to go to Korea on business. Nora felt sad, but they arranged to email each other. They concluded their meal and left for home. Nora felt as if her world was falling apart. Her escape route was her diary before she went to bed. Her plan the following day was to check the outside kitchen garden which had not been looked at and seemed to have potential.

Saturday morning came around quickly. She went outside and looked at the wild garden. Armed with her notebook, she planned what she would do with it. She wanted to create a small flower and herb garden and an alcove for her to work in. She would chat to the builders about her ideas. This took her mind off Alan. She phoned Anita and they went for coffee. Nora told her about Alan heading to Korea for three weeks. Nora and Alan emailed each other until Alan returned home.

Hi Alan darling,

I really miss you, and I see you are hard at work. I have made progress in the refurbishing of the old house and the grounds. I went with the builder to the old cottage to take a look at it. Tom Chrisom wants to buy it, so Mr Hanks will contact you when you return to your office to arrange a sale. I told the builder that Tom wants to put his own ideas into the new design. It has come a long way now, but until Tom sees the builder, the building work will remain at a standstill. When the builder and I were leaving the cottage, I noticed the child ghost walking in a straight line to the old oak tree. I was puzzled, so I asked the builder to come with me to view the tree and the tree house. Also I wanted to see what the child ghost was up to. I discovered a footpath leading from the cottage but it was covered in weeds.

The tree house is in bad repair, so the builder said he could do a job on it. I gave him the go-ahead. I headed back to the old house, and again the child ghost followed me, but this time he disappeared between two bushes, so I decided to see what was behind them. I found some steps leading down to a door. I had not noticed this before. I could not believe that a key was stuck in the lock. To my surprise there was a lot of stuff in the basement, which I have made a start on clearing out. The old house is being resurrected from decay to a new life! I can't wait to see you!

Love, Nora.

Hi Nora,

Your email gave me a great thrill. I miss you a great deal too. I see you have had a busy time supervising the building work. It has been a rough time for all of us. I am looking forward to my return home and to seeing at all the improvements that have taken place. I am sure Tom the gardener will be pleased with his cottage and his grandchildren will love the tree house. I had a sudden thought though – did you search the tree house to see if anything from the previous owners was left behind?

Here in Korea, I have had two occasions to sell some new houses which came on the market, resulting in two families having their own space. They have a novel way of building their homes. My friends have invited us out here for a holiday sometime. I told them I would think about it. What do you think of the idea of coming here?
See you next week, darling.

Alan. Xxx

Nora and Anita had decided to take time out for a coffee and went to the café. Nora told her about Alan's emails and how she missed him. Anita asked her if she had told Alan about the ghost and the dress.

Nora replied, 'Yes to the ghost and no about the dress. I have hidden it under his nose.'

They left the café, and Anita returned to work. Nora went for a walk around the perimeter of the land inside the boundaries of the old house. She would check the grounds that needed clearing. On her way she noticed a pathway which seemed to lead to the cottage and the oak tree. She followed this path, and as she turned around she had a very clear view of the house. It was beautiful in the sunshine, and then she noticed her ghost friend was following her, but as she went back around the opposite way, he disappeared. She went in the direction of where he had disappeared to investigate further. She arrived at the side of the house and noticed a door which seemed to come up from the basement. She presumed the Gardaí had not noticed it either. It was locked. She paid another visit to the basement to try to find the door she had discovered from the garden side. After a lot of searching, Nora found the door hidden behind what seemed like a wall made of plywood. The key was still in the lock, and with some difficulty she managed to open it. It led through into another room off the basement. She was interrupted by the sound of her phone ringing upstairs. She hurried up, concerned that it was Alan. It was. He told her he was nearly finished with his work in Korea and would be home soon.

'What has been happening with you?' he asked.

Nora told him about the door leading down to the basement from the outside and how busy she had been since he was away. They said their goodbyes. Nora was looking forward to his return from Korea. It surprised her how much she missed him.

Happy with herself, she went to prepare a meal and write in her diary.

The next day Nora informed Detective Chrisom about the outside door in the basement. Searching through the newly found room off the basement, he found another trunk. Somebody must have packed in a hurry, he thought.

'Did Rita find out anything about the original gardener?' he asked Nora.

'I have not yet heard,' Nora replied.

Nora went to the hotel to be alone to reflect on all that had happened. The waitress came and took her order.

'A penny for your thoughts,' a voice said, as Alan put his hand on her chair.

Nora came out of her reverie. Recognising the voice, she jumped up and gave the astounded Alan a big hug.

'When did you get back?' she asked.

'Half an hour ago,' he replied, laughing.

'Welcome home. I have missed you. Update me with all that has gone on,' she said.

'It is a long story. Let's chat about it over dinner tomorrow night,' Alan said.

When coffee was finished, she went back to the old house, and he went home.

Nora dressed up for the following evening. Alan collected her at seven o'clock and headed to the next town of Notertent. Over the meal he told her he had gone to Korea to put the final closure to his business. He wouldn't be returning for a while.

'What kind of business?' she asked.

'I had an auctioneering business,' he replied. 'It closed down because the competition was very strong. I have friends out in Korea, and I wanted to let them know that I would not be returning. I have a wonderful life here with you, Nora,' he said.

Nora blushed nervously.

Oblivious to all others, he took a black ring box from his pocket, got down on one knee and opened it. 'Nora, will you marry me?' he asked.

Tears flowed down her face as she said, 'I will marry you, and I love you, Alan.'

She was not aware of other people until she heard the clapping. Anita and Mr Hanks arrived at their table with a bouquet of flowers and congratulated them. Alan had arranged for them to be there, and they all moved to a larger table. The meal and the evening went really well. On leaving the restaurant, Alan and Nora walked down by the canal as it was a lovely evening.

'When did you arrange all this?' she asked him.

'I booked the meal a month ago but only asked Anita and Mr Hanks to join us yesterday. It has been the longest month I have ever put in,' he told her. He kissed her passionately on the lips when they arrived at the old house, and he said goodnight at the door.

'Thank you for asking me. I love you,' said Nora, before kissing him again. 'I'll see you tomorrow.'

Nora went inside. Instead of going to her room, she went to the kitchen for a glass of water. She cried with a mixture of happiness and excitement. Suddenly she felt a touch like a feather on her arm. Her little ghost child spoke to her and said, 'Don't cry!' Nora knew that she could hear him, but it was the first time he had spoken. She told him what had happened, but he just smiled and disappeared.

The following day she phoned Anita and arranged to meet for lunch at the hotel.

'Congratulations!' Anita said again and gave her a huge bear hug. Both of them were crying with happiness. She told Anita about the second surprise of the evening: the ghost child had spoken to her. Anita was surprised also and expressed relief that the ghost seemed friendly, at least.

Nora asked Alan if they could arrange an evening meal for their friends to tell them the good news. It was arranged for the following week. In the meantime, Nora spoke to her family and Alan to his. Nora and Alan decided to travel to Nora's family that weekend and to Alan's the following weekend.

Nora started the wedding preparations. Her first priority was to check if the wedding dress she had found in the basement could be cleaned, so she took it into town to the dry cleaners and explained her dilemma. The assistant told her that it could have special treatment and that steam cleaning it would be the safest option in this case.

The day for the meal with their friends arrived. Nora arranged to have Tom Chrisom, her soon-to-be new gardener, Rita her researcher and Peggy the housekeeper to join them as well. Alan and Nora gave them all the good news. During the meal Nora asked Rita how the research was going. So far, everything she had found, they knew about. She was still trying to find the original gardener and the family of the child. Tom told them the investigation was winding down, and they could begin to refurbish the top floor. Nora was delighted with this news. The evening drew to a close, and everyone had a great time. Nora and Alan remained and planned the weekend ahead.

They left for Kilkenny on Saturday morning to visit Nora's family. On arriving in the city, they booked into the Ormond Hotel. Nora decided that a family meal would be most appropriate. They all met in the lounge. With the introductions and liquid refreshments over, they headed to the restaurant. Nora had been nervous, but she felt Alan was accepted and the meal went very well. There was only one flaw to the evening: her mother was in a nursing home recuperating after a small operation and could not join them. After the meal, Nora and Alan decided to visit the nursing home and spend time with her. Alan spent time chatting with her, explaining he was an estate agent and living in Latimore. The afternoon went quickly, and Nora and Alan left as it was mealtime for her mother. That evening they went to a musical night in Kettler's Inn close to their hotel. The band were cousins of Nora's. It was a very enjoyable evening as the whole extended family was there. All were given the news of Nora's engagement.

Back at the hotel they went to bed and slept soundly. The next morning they attended the Franciscan Friary for Sunday Mass. Afterwards they went to a local restaurant for lunch and then returned to Latimore. Nora had a happy weekend and had time to sort out some wedding plans. One of her key priorities was to see if it was possible to get her mother to the wedding. Nora's brother said he would see to that.

Monday morning arrived all too quickly, and it was back to sorting out the house and the new staff. Nora arranged to meet Rita and Anita that evening to assess how the research was going and to let them know about the weekend. Rita informed them that she had found the previous gardener in a nursing home in Kilkenny. He had been a gardener for twenty years and worked on the garden in the old house. Rita had made arrangements for them to visit him. They planned to travel to meet him on Wednesday. Anita said she would arrange to take the day off, and they could set off early. When the evening was over the friends went home, but Nora decided to write in her diary. She phoned Alan to tell him about the original gardener of the old house. He offered to drive them all down to Kilkenny.

Wednesday dawned, and the friends met at the old house. Alan picked them up. The journey down was uneventful. They arrived at the nursing home and went in to the reception area where they met the matron and the ward sister. The gardener was in a room on his own. Nora requested that a nurse would stay in case they needed help. The friends were introduced to Sean Peek, the previous gardener of the old house for twenty years. He was very weak even though the back of the bed was up and he was propped up with pillows to support his back. He told them he had a story that he wanted to share with them. All of them sat down and faced the elderly man.

'My employer, Mr McNamara, went looking for a gardener to care for his large garden. I did my apprenticeship in the large McCalmount Estate, and I was looking for work. I accepted his offer of a good wage plus a cottage on the grounds. I had to trim all the trees and landscape the land as often as required. At my suggestion he leased two fields out to local farmers. Mr McNamara left the work to me, as he did not have much knowledge.

'His young wife had a garden for her own use at the back of the kitchen for herbs and vegetables. Life settled down. The husband was away a lot, and the young wife was lonely. They had a baby boy, and the mother doted on him. He used to play in the front lawn – a lovely blonde little lad. His dad came home one evening from work, and built a tree house for him. He enjoyed watching and playing with his precious little boy. One day when he came home from work, the child was not to be seen. He asked where the child was and his wife told him he was in bed asleep.

'When the father arrived in the child's room to say goodnight, he was shocked and frightened to find that his son was dead. Mr McNamara guessed his wife had done something to cause the death of the child. The local doctor was called and told them it appeared to be a cot death. He urged them to call the Gardaí. Mr McNamara did not do this. No Gardaí were called. Instead, he asked me to build a room around the dead child. I strongly suggested to him that he call the Gardaí, and I refused to build the room. Mr McNamara built the room himself.

'A few hours later, he gave me my notice and a month's wages. I found a smaller job of gardening here at this home, and when I got too old to live alone, I moved in. I have kept this story to myself for twenty years. I am so glad to have it off my chest,' he told them.

Nora decided to tell him about finding the skeleton of a young child in a room within a room.

'I am glad that now this little boy can finally be put to rest properly,' he said.

Sean was beginning to feel tired, and the nurse said it was time to go. They said their goodbyes and thanked him for his story. He asked if the Gardaí would be visiting him. Nora said they wouldn't be. She would explain the story to them on his behalf, and he need not worry. He thanked her and said that now he could die happy, but he had something else to say.

'There is a diary in the little desk in the tree house and another in the child's room,' said the old gardener. He was sure there must be other diaries, but he did not know where they were. 'The young Mrs McNamara wrote a lot. Maybe she was alone too much,' he added.

They thanked him for his time and left. They went to the local hotel for a meal and decided that Rita should write Sean Peek's story down. Nora decided she would tell Detective Tom all about it the next day.

When they arrived home, Nora's phone was ringing. It was the matron calling to say that Sean Peek had just died. She told Nora that it had been a great relief for him to tell his story. She had done him a great service. Nora thanked her and felt very sad, as she would have loved to know more about the personalities of the young McNamara couple.

The next morning Rita came in to catalogue the library. While clearing a lower shelf she found a box of papers. She opened them to discover that they included the marriage certificate of Mr and Mrs McNamara and the baptismal certificate of the child. Nora was pleased, as she now had a name for the ghost child. She explained this to Rita, and they waited for the child to appear and see if he would respond to his name. In the kitchen over coffee, Rita told her how much progress she had made on the young family, who had purchased the house from an old English family of Pembrokeshire in Wales. Rita collected the box of papers and went back to the library. Nora headed into her office to review the progress on the building. The Gardaí had gone, so now the builders were coming in to clear both rooms and make it an en-suite.

Suddenly, while she was working, her little ghost child appeared. She called out his name, 'Hello, little Tom,' and she smiled at him.

He smiled back and clapped his hands. He caught her by the hand and led her upstairs to the room where the skeleton had been found. Nora felt apprehensive about entering the room. There was a little cupboard at the back of the bed. She opened it and there she found a collection of handwritten diary notebooks. It seemed his mother had written them. The ghost child disappeared once Nora held the diaries in her hand, and she went downstairs to her office to read them. Soon she came across the entries that revealed the true nature of the child's death, and it was truly heartbreaking. It was not a cot death after all, but infanticide. Nora read Mrs McNamara's words carefully:

> I am fed up listening to little Tom who has been crying all day. I feel so alone during the day when his father is at work. He travels so much. I feel I am a bad mother and little Tom would be better off without me. If only Tom senior could see how I am struggling. I put little Tom to bed. When he finally settled down, I waited for a few minutes to make sure he was fast asleep. Watching him sleep, I felt so overwhelmed. I need my life back. I took a pillow and

placed it over his face. He reacted but after a while he became very still. I shook with fear at what I had just done. When his father came home he asked for little Tom. I said he was sleeping, but he decided to check on him. Tom senior came downstairs and called the doctor. He told me little Tom was dead. I went into convulsions. The doctor came and gave me a sedative to calm me down. He went to see little Tom and confirmed the death. He did not call the Gardaí but strongly encouraged my husband to do so. I was the only one who knew the truth. Tom comforted me as best he knew how. I had to tell him the real truth and how desperate I was. He asked Sean the gardener if he would build a room around our son, but Sean suggested we call the Gardaí. My husband decided to build the room himself. We had planned to leave on holiday, but now things have changed. He knows we have to flee and has instructed me to pack my bags. I know we will not return to this old house ever again. We will leave the past and our son behind.

Nora cried for the young couple and phoned Detective Tom to tell him about the visit to the nursing home and the death of the gardener. She also offered him the diaries with details outlining the death of the child.

'Yes, I will call over to collect them. I'll return them when I have read them unless it will help us find the parents of little Tom,' he replied.

CHAPTER FOUR

———◆———

NORA HOPED RITA COULD FIND out why little Tom's mother was driven to kill him. She wondered where his parents were now, if they were still alive. It was so long ago. When Detective Tom returned the diaries, she gave them to Rita and asked if it was possible to find out what really happened. Maybe the library archives might have an article on the house or the couple. As the husband was a seasoned traveller he may have had a house abroad. Rita told her that she would try the travel agents and the heritage sites on the internet to see if she could come up with anything.

Nora decided that a walk would be an ideal way to calm down. She went out to visit the old cottage and check on the builders' progress. She found no one around so she took a good look and knew that the builders were doing a good job of refurbishing it. Some of it was still unfinished as Detective Tom was going to put his own touch to it. She headed to the old tree and tree house. She did not climb into it, as it was too rickety for her. She had asked the builder to fix it up in memory of the ghost child, little Tom, and to bring down the old desk for her. She opened it to find the diary hidden inside. She took it to add to the others.

On her way back to the old house, she looked up at the windows. They were all accounted for now. Peggy, her housekeeper, came to meet her to plan the housekeeping duties, time off and holidays. Nora and Peggy went into her office. While there, little Tom came in and Nora smiled. Peggy wondered why she was smiling all of a sudden. It was then that little Tom decided to reveal himself to Peggy, who got a fright.

'My God, that child's face is familiar!' Peggy stammered.

'So now that you have seen him, why is he familiar?' Nora asked her.

'I knew about the ghost like everybody in the town, but no one had seen him. His mother used to come into our shop for her groceries. My mother served Mrs McNamara on many occasions,' Peggy said.

When Nora asked if Peggy's mother was still alive, Peggy confirmed that she was.

'Would it be OK with you if Rita, my researcher, spoke to your mother? Perhaps she will remember something useful about the McNamara family.'

'I don't see why not,' Peggy replied. 'I will ask her this evening and maybe you both could come over tomorrow evening.'

Nora told Peggy about the forthcoming wedding and asked if the reception could be combined with the housewarming party at the old house. Peggy was over the moon and happily agreed to plan everything. Alan phoned and asked to come and see her. Nora agreed. When Alan arrived, he told her about their plans for the weekend with his parents. Nora was delighted and told him about her discovery that Peggy's mother knew the young Mrs McNamara. She explained that Peggy was going to ask if they could visit with Peggy's mother tomorrow evening.

'Would you like to come with us?' Nora asked.

'Yes I would, as I know Peggy's mother. It will be a pleasure to see her again,' Alan said.

'Now that we are here, I have a suggestion for you!' Nora said. 'I have been thinking and wondered if you would like to move your office into the old house and save expense.'

'I will think about it. It would be a great idea,' Alan replied. Before taking his leave, he arranged to meet Nora and Rita the next day at Peggy's house.

Rita was going home too but informed Nora that she would be in tomorrow early to type up the history of the family. She would then start on the history of the house itself. Nora was delighted.

She told Rita that they were going to visit Peggy's mother to find out more about the family. Left alone, she started writing about her day. Nora began to feel nervous about the weekend. Would Alan's family accept her? Would they like her?

The time arrived to visit Peggy's mother. Peggy led them into a nice warm kitchen where tea and scones were laid out on top of a lovely white tablecloth. They sat down and asked what she could remember of Mrs McNamara.

'Well! She was a slim tall lady. She liked fresh food. She never bought anything in a tin. This surprised me as tinned food is handy in an emergency. She never stayed to have a chat with anyone in the shop. She gave the impression that she was above the rest of us. It seemed strange. I used to call her "the ice maiden" but knew she was married and had a son,' Peggy's mother said.

As she offered them more tea, she continued. 'One day when she was shopping she said she was going away on a holiday with the family. The next thing we heard was that the family had gone. Even their gardener left and got another job in Kilkenny. I always wondered what had happened to them.'

Nora looked at Peggy and at the faces of the others sitting around the table. She decided to tell them what had happened to the child and the diaries of the incident.

'May God rest him,' Peggy's mum said when Nora had finished recounting the tragic story. 'We still do not know where the parents are now.'

After an hour of chatting they left Peggy's home and returned to the old house. This story matched what had been written in the diaries. Everyone agreed to go for a drink before calling it a day. Nora and Alan told the others they would be away for the weekend in the midlands visiting his parents.

The weekend approached, and they set off on Friday evening. This time they decided to stay in the Court Hotel. An evening drink with some members of the family went well. The next morning they went to meet Alan's mother who was confined to her home due to old age. The day passed off very well, and a review of the wedding plans was a great success. Sunday morning arrived and after Mass they had a meal with the family and left for home.

Nora was pleased with her weekend, as she felt accepted by all of Alan's family.

At home, they went for a walk around the grounds and viewed the house without the builders. Alan asked Nora if she was sure that he could move his office into the old house. She was sure. He accepted and told her that he would instruct the builders to rearrange the front room to the left of the entrance. Nora headed to her office to sort out the wedding arrangements with Alan. This was a fine ending to a good weekend.

As Nora was meeting Anita, Rita and Peggy the next day, she put her wedding plans into action. They made arrangements for the reception, the bridesmaids, the best man and groomsmen. She was getting excited and nervous. A visit to her diary was now essential. As she opened her diary, she thought about little Tom's mother who also drew great comfort writing in a diary. She appeared to have no friends, unlike Nora who had plenty of true friends.

The wedding date was approaching. Nora and her bridesmaids went for a dress fitting. She had her own wedding dress fitted, and it was perfect. Even the veil was long enough to wear down her back. When she had opened the old box, she had also discovered a matching bolero jacket. Nora was surprised everything fitted so well. She went to check the flowers she had chosen: white and velvet roses. When the fittings were over, Nora and her friends went for a meal. She imagined the young Mrs McNamara as the same height and weight as herself. They all returned to the house and had coffee while going over the wedding ceremony.

Nora had prepared the Mass and the singing. The local parish priest helped her with the updated liturgy. She decided on three candles in the centre of the altar to represent the couple becoming one. There were two readings, one from the book of Proverbs and the other from the Gospel of John. With this done, everyone went home apart from Rita who had a few things to finish up in the library. Nora went to her office to organise some final touches to the wedding.

Nora kept her diary in her bedroom, and she decided to write her thoughts on little Tom and his parents. There was still no news about whether they were dead or alive. Suddenly little Tom came in, sat down and waited for her to stop writing. Feeling his presence, she looked up and smiled at him. He took her hand and brought her to a door at the end of the bedroom where he had died. Nora felt very sad and frightened going into this room. She did not know why, as she had little Tom beside her. She overcame her fear and went in. The builders had done a good job removing the inner room and had made it into an en-suite. Tom led her into a corner. He was looking for something. Nora tapped the entire wall. It felt hollow just where they were standing. The builders had left some tools behind, so she picked up a chisel and bore a hole into the wall. It seemed to be a cupboard. Little Tom said, 'It is in a box.'

Nora used her flash lamp and indeed she found a box where one would keep a diary. This one was well hidden. Little Tom disappeared, and Nora went downstairs. Rita was coming out of the library, and Nora showed her the boxed diary. They lifted it out of its box and opened it. It had house plans, drawings and personal notes. This seemed to belong to Mr McNamara. They detailed his plans for the garden and a lovely one for the kitchen. Nora noticed he had written the address of where they were moving to. Nora was delighted and phoned Detective Tom who said he would inquire with his colleague in Scotland Yard, but it would take some time. Nora left the boxed diary with Rita and suggested she copy the garden plans and give them to Detective Tom who was also her new gardener. Maybe he would landscape the kitchen garden and build an alcove for her. The builders should soon be finished in the cottage.

The eve of the wedding arrived, and Nora had to go with Alan and all the family for a practice. Brothers on both sides of the family were reading. They took their places near the reading lectern. The bride's family sat on the left of the church and the groom's family on the right. The groom and the best man stood at the front of the altar. Nora walked up the aisle on the arm of her brother, behind her bridesmaids. It went well and according to plan. They would sign the registrar at the side of the altar.

Before the wedding they had decided on no hen or stag

parties but a family meal. After a long day, Nora visited her diary before bed.

The sun rose high in the sky, and the dawn was spectacular. Nora got up and went for her usual walk. For the first time she was alone. Little Tom was not with her, and for some reason she felt lonely. Anita and Rita joined her, and both noticed her sadness. Returning after the walk, they helped her get into her dress and did her hair and make-up. At last they were ready. The photographer had arrived and was setting up. The first photo was Nora holding her bouquet, followed by one with her bridesmaids in front of the old house. He also took a photo of her friends at the bottom of the stairs. The open-top car arrived, and Nora and her brother left for the church. A limo came for the bridesmaids

The ceremony in the church went very well, and it was emotional for both sides. For Alan's parents, it seemed like a dream come true. Family photos were taken outside the church, and it was back to the old house for the reception. In the car on the way back, the newlyweds spoke happily together.

'You're the most beautiful bride today. The dress is magnificent and suits you perfectly,' Alan said.

She explained her discovery of the dress and where it was hidden, and they briefly discussed little Tom. Nora told him about her diary find in the room where the child had died and that Detective Tom was asking his colleague in Scotland Yard to see if the parents were still alive.

'Well, we will let the guests have a tour of the old house after the meal and then we will go to the airport,' said Alan.

'Where are we going?' asked Nora.

'I am taking you to see my friends in Korea. They could not come over for the wedding, so I promised I would take you to them. That is why I wanted to take care of the honeymoon,' he said.

They arrived at the old house. It seemed to be alive, as if new life had just entered. They arrived up the avenue to a rapturous welcome of family and friends. Peggy and her staff had excelled themselves. Nora whispered something to Alan and both nodded to each other.

The Old House

The meal was superb. Speeches were given and the good-wish cards of those who could not come were read. A beautiful gift arrived for Alan and Nora, so they opened it there and then. It was a wedding candle set, with their names and the date engraved in silver. They displayed it on the centre table near the cake. The photographer took photos of the top table and of their guests. Photos were also taken of the centre piece and the cutting of the cake. Alan invited the guests to take a tour of the house with Rita guiding them. Nora and Alan thanked Peggy for the wonderful meal, said their goodbyes and left for the airport while their family and friends danced the night away.

While Nora and Alan were in Korea, the old house and the grounds were a hive of activity. Peggy and Rita redesigned the downstairs rooms. They turned the first room into a reception area and the second room into Alan's new office. His secretary, Ann Boson, brought over all the office equipment and files. They turned the third room into an en-suite leading into Alan and Nora's bedroom. The library was catalogued and reconditioned to protect the books. The front of the old house was also decorated to welcome them home. Detective Tom had finished the cottage and was planning to move in at the end of the month with his wife, Maria. The tree house could now be used safely.

The builders had the upstairs near conclusion. They opened the hole in little Tom's room that Nora had made and pulled down the partition. Behind it they revealed a beautiful carved panelled wall. Behind the wooden panelling there was a small room, like a private office of some kind. Rita went in search of the house plans to see if this room had been drawn in. It was decided that they would wait until Nora and Alan could decide what to use this new room for. Nora and Alan were due home the next day and everything was in order. Unbeknownst to all who had worked tirelessly as the newlyweds were away, little Tom appeared every evening when the house fell empty. He roamed around to see all the changes to the house. His little room had changed but he was happy.

The Old House

The day of the honeymooners' return dawned. Anita, Rita, Mr Hanks and their friends were all waiting as the taxi drove up the avenue. Nora marvelled at how beautiful her old house looked. She could not dwell on it, as the noise of the welcome party was distracting. They got out of the taxi and stood looking in amazement at all the people. It was a very emotional and wonderful sight.

Everyone went inside for drinks and to hear the news of their trip. When two hours had passed, everyone left except Anita, Rita and Peggy. Excitedly, they told Nora and Alan that they had something to show them, and they all climbed the stairs. They showed them the room behind the wooden panelling in little Tom's room. Nora still felt apprehensive entering, but with Alan by her side it felt easier. It was so different with the carved wooden panelling leading into a small room. Both Alan and Nora stood still in amazement. Rita informed them the walls had hidden the room which was not drawn into the house plans. Rita and Peggy also showed them Alan's new office. His secretary, Ann, would be in first thing in the morning. Rita, Anita and Peggy left, and after a nightcap, Nora and Alan went to bed.

At dawn the next day, Nora was out walking. She noticed the land was taking on a different shape. Returning, she asked Alan if he could walk around with her, which he did after breakfast. Standing by the front door, they saw that the path had been cleared, and primroses were shooting up along the walkway. It would be a lovely yellow flower patch. Inside the house, it was bright, warm and sunny. They returned to the new hidden room. They stood looking at the little room but could not make out what it had been used for. Nora went down to the kitchen and out to the garden. There for the first time she laid eyes on the most beautiful conservatory and alcove. The builders had excelled themselves. She could be alone here to do her writing.

As the staff arrived, Rita spoke to her about the research on the family, her uncle and the ghost child which she had ready in a manuscript form.

'Do you want to publish it?' she asked Nora.

'Yes, I plan to, once I see how it reads,' Nora replied.

Nora headed to the library and was very pleased at the way it had been refurbished.

'My uncle would be delighted at the way you have done this,' she said to Rita.

Anita joined them to discuss house insurance. Mr Hanks had sent over names of recommended insurers for Nora to browse through. While Alan was working in his office, the friends went walking around the grounds. They visited the cottage and to see new life in it was lovely. The tree house was ready to use. Nora thought that Detective Tom's grandchildren would have a ball in there, and she considered giving it to him.

They returned to the old house and had coffee in the sitting room. Alan and his secretary Ann joined them. There suddenly seemed to be a cold air in the room. Nora remembered this from the first time the little ghost had appeared to her. She thought of Alan's secretary, who had never seen the ghost, and her possible reaction.

'You have not seen our ghost, Ann, have you?' Nora said.

'No,' Ann replied.

Just then little Tom appeared. He took Nora by the hand and led her out of the room, which was unusual. Outside of the room there stood a man and a woman. He told her the young couple were his mum and dad. He wanted to show them to the others. Nora couldn't believe her eyes. She felt totally honoured that little Tom wanted her to meet his parents. Nora went into the room to warn the others before opening the door for the ghosts of the McNamara family to enter.

'Thank you for believing in Tom. I know you have read my diaries and know my story. I want to ask you to remember me with kindness and compassion,' Mrs McNamara said to Nora.

Mr McNamara came forward and shook hands with Nora. He informed them that the little room had been his private office in the winter time. 'Don't leave your wife alone for long. Loneliness can be a terrible thing,' he said to Alan.

They thanked Nora and disappeared. Nora knew instinctively

that this was the last time she would ever see little Tom again. He had finally been reunited with his parents. A shocked audience sat in the sitting room, speechless at what they had just witnessed.

Nora sat on the wooden bench under the beech tree in her back garden. Alan Ladd had gone to his office, and life appeared normal. It was not always so for Nora. She remembered how life had been such a roller coaster for the last few years. It started with her moving to Latimore and her daily jogging. Her past life was just that, past history. She had something in common with the old house. It was once old and dilapidated, but now it was transformed and redesigned. The ghost of little Tom and his parents were laid to rest. New life had begun for Nora, Alan, and the old house with its new title of 'Our House'.

CARTOONS

A personal selection of his cartoons from *The Times* and
The Listener introduced and selected by
BARRY FANTONI

GW00514768

CARTOONS

BARRY FANTONI

A STAR BOOK
published by
the Paperback Division of
W.H. ALLEN & Co. PLC

A Star Book
Published in 1987
by the Paperback Division of
W.H. Allen & Co. PLC
44 Hill Street, London W1X 8LB

Copyright © Barry Fantoni 1987

Typeset by Avocet Marketing Services, Bicester, Oxon.
Printed and bound in Great Britain by
Anchor Brendon Ltd, Tiptree, Essex

ISBN 0 352 32114 8

Introduction

Although I have been on *The Times Diary* for five years, and working for *The Listener* for an uninterrupted 20, the cartoons I have selected for this collection are taken from a period of roughly three years. Jokes quickly grow stale and the choice of what to put in and what to leave out is never easy. The rule of thumb I use is quite simply whether or not the cartoon still amuses me. On the whole, the selection before you has that quality. The cartoons I chose might not be about a very important event [often the funniest are inspired by the most insignificant news story] but as long as there was still at least the echo of a laugh it got in.

Whenever possible I have tried to include jokes which are particular favourites. I firmly believe that a crucial factor in judging something as personal as a joke must in the end rest upon individual taste. In my experience, all attempts to arrive at humour through communal debate are doomed. As with all things, by trying to please everyone, you end up pleasing no one.

The cartoons I do for *The Times* are slightly different from those I contribute to *The Listener*. *The Times* is a daily routine. I read the paper early, about seven o clock, and once I have cleared the caption with the editor on duty I get on and draw up the finished product. I never do roughs or change cartoons. If a drawing goes badly I tear it up and start again. This way I feel my work has both the immediacy and freshness a daily cartoon requires in order to make its point effectively.

The Listener operates in a quite different way. Whereas *The Times* demands I keep my eye sharply focused on hard news, *The Listener* has a softer approach. Here I can be just a little less topical and draw my subjects from a broader source. Because *The Listener* is essentially a broadcasting paper, I can comment on those stories which are about radio and TV with greater freedom. The cartoon on the cover, for example, comes from

The Listener – it sat better on their diary page than it would have in *The Times*.

In the three years that are covered by the cartoons published here, we have had a general election, seen an end to the long running miner's strike, watched football hooliganism reach new levels and been witnesses to a thousand tiny stories that make up the fabric of our lives. In my view there are areas into which cartoonists should refrain from stepping – no matter how strongly they feel, or how effective they think their joke might be. Terrorist bomb attacks are one such taboo; sickness and disasters are two others. Yet I find there are a number of cartoonists who show no such personal censorship. Those who might find lack of stereotypes and racist humour in my work have both my apology and sympathy.

As the luck of the draw has it, I am the only cartoonist in Britain who works for a quality daily and produces a cartoon for every edition: six a week, 50 weeks a year. My work for *The Times* numbers a total of almost 1,500 jokes, and *The Listener* is in the region of 1,000. When laid end to end my originals wouldn't reach from John O' Groats to Lands End, but they would paper the average family fall out shelter. I enjoyed the task of looking through my envelopes filled with what I regard as old friends and dusting down those I felt might give you, the reader, a bit of a chuckle. I hope I have succeeded.

Barry Fantoni
July 1987

'Do you think anyone will notice?'

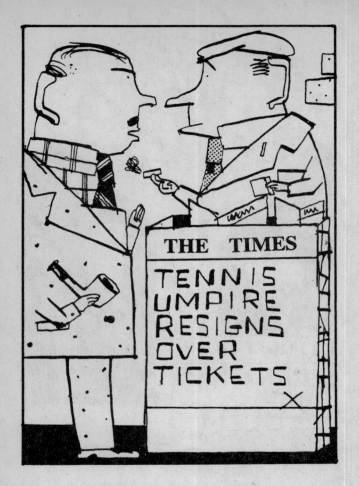

'Apparently he asked for another
3,270 line calls to be taken into
consideration'

'Dalek, you were wonderful'

'I hope we're not in for another spate
of pyramid selling'

'It's Cezanne's still life with frozen
fish finger'

'Man, that's a lot of money for a
smoke-filled basement'

'Wonderful news. Our fall-out shelter
has been listed as a Grade 2 building'

'I'm a sort of arms manufacturer –
I make seats for soccer stadiums'

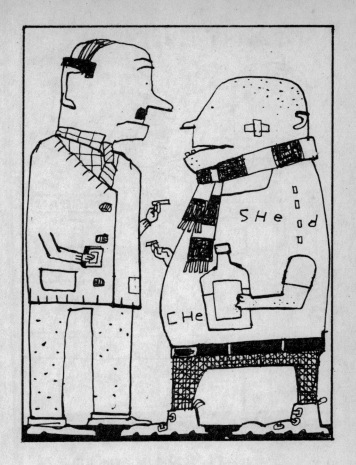

'I'm off to the match: see you in
five years'

'We might be forced into uniform,
Hopkins, but remember mine's the
rice bowl with the willow pattern'

'Have you got "The Secret Diary of
Sara Keays. Aged 38¾?"'

'Would you like to drive back to the
pub for another couple of pints?
This intoximeter isn't working
properly'

"Nothing here for 'It's a fair cop, guv,
I'll come quietly.'"

'It's the last bottle of Austrian:
nip out and drain the car radiator'

'And now 800 million fans are
running onto the pitch'

'Apparently their policy paper is
printed on recycled manifestos'

'Muggers kicked the door in on
Tuesday night. Police kicked it in
again last night looking for them'

'I saw one gunman. He had hair the colour of ripe cornfields... eyes the blue of a summer sky'

'The minute they call, Neville's going
to lock himself in the fall-out shelter'

'It's not my husband coming home
early that worries me, it's the
children'

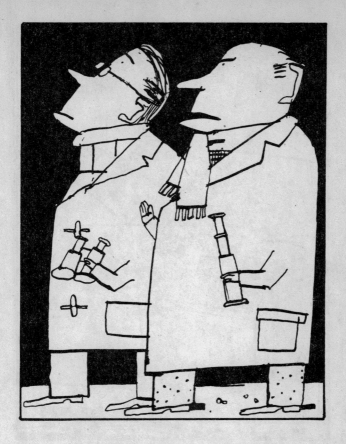

'I wish Halley's Comet would shift
out of the way, I'm trying to see the
space shuttle'

'Good heavens! Another previously
undiscovered Shakespeare poem'

'Perhaps it's a move to keep stately
homes open late'

'If I can't find you a window seat,
would sitting by a crack do?

'Cold? Not me. Someone always pops
in from the GLC and throws some
money on the fire'

'Great... it shows more animation
than the real thing'

'Another great year for us – we
handle Kleenex tissues'

'Jeremy and Ralph are hoping to buy
the room they met in and turn it
into a flat'

'What rhymes with "My husband and I"?'

'Don't smile'

'I've got a job in the Atlantic picking
up bits of Branson's speedboat'

'Now I know why they call her the
girl next door... that's where most
of my letters go'

'I hear the latest idea is to equip
warheads with radioactive lamb'

'Pity one of them had to win'

'Remind me, does it mean Michael
Caine is coming or going?'

'Neville was about to bid when
someone hit him with a custard pie'

'Passengers to the aircraft's left can
just see the residents of Hounslow
shaking their fists'

'No water, old man – watching my
radiation levels . . .'

'I appreciate your caution, darling,
but an hour and a half every
four years . . .'

'To the Editor of the Times:'
"Dear Sir, I have just seen my first
soccer hooligan . . ."'

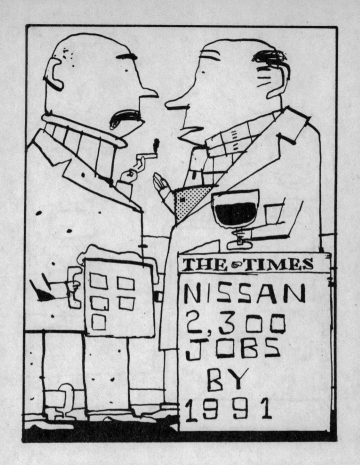

'Great! Unemployment will be solved
by the year 3290'

'Apparently the idea is to pay
Terry Wogan directly'

'I was queueing to pay twenty-four
quid for speeding and got a parking
ticket'

'Must be funny seeing a telly that's
never had Terry Wogan on it'

'I understand they refused an initial
offer of TV licence stamps'

'Does that mean we've spent all
that money on a private education
for nothing?'

'The good news is that your hotel
has been built. The bad news is that
it's been blown up by a bomb'

'I see they've still kept the
Birmingham road map'

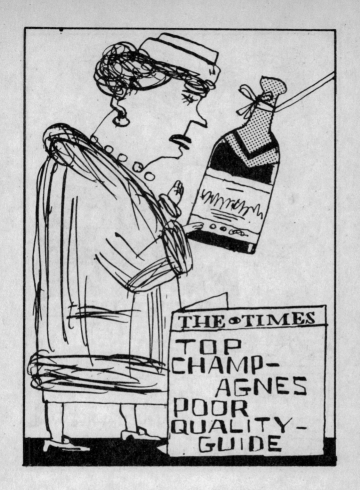

'I name this ship – Good Heavens,
This Stuff's Undrinkable . . .'

'My client's evidence, M'lud, will be
arriving at 9.57, 10.32 and 11.58'

'So when I saw these two conductors,
I said to myself, lay off the interval
drink.'

'Mine's too tired even to make
excuses'

'How come *you* never see anything?'

'It started out as a hangover and
ended up as designer stubble'

'Funny going back with a chap and
actually seeing his etchings'

'What are we running short of –
judges or chemists?'

'Interesting bit here on the number
of directors to resign in a year'

'What's the point of vandalizing a
phone kiosk if it doesn't work?'

'No time to get to know each other,
I'm only in for rape'

'Does that mean we have to wear
gas masks?'

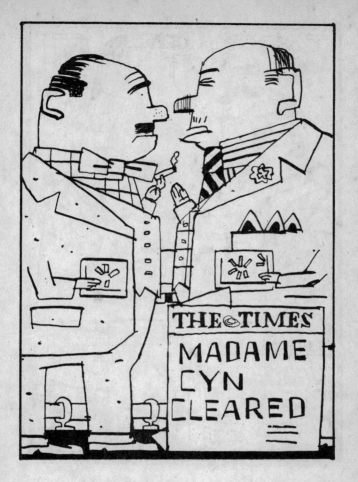

'Cheer up, old man, there must be
dozens of genuine places'

'Surely the charm of Greek music
is that it *does* all sound the same'

'Yes, and I love Dior's tractor suit
with matching accessories'

'And when asked who chopped down
the cherry tree, Ronald Reagan said,
I can't remember'

'Looks like one for the Pools Panel'

'Apparently the stumbling-block is
Sizewell B'

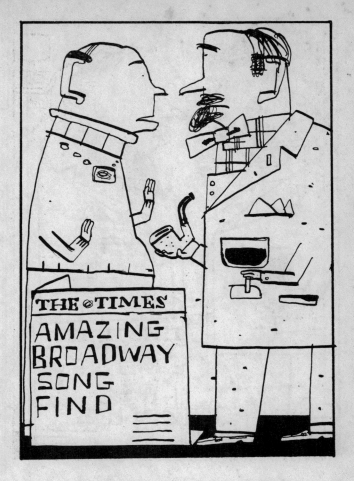

'Just think. Now we can be nostalgic
about tunes we've never heard'

'I admit, Gerald, I do admire you
for giving up'

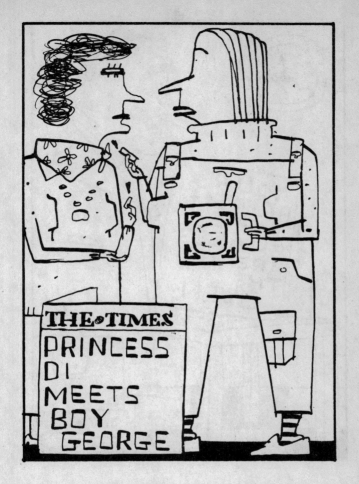

'Apparently he gave her the name of
his dressmaker'

'I know it's confusing but A.A. Milne
also lived in a world of make-believe'

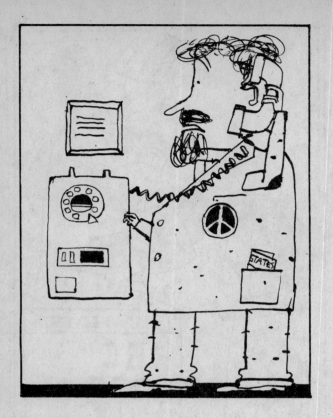

'Hello, operator? My wife and I were
talking to MI5 and got cut off'

'I must warn you, anything you say
will be taken down and may be used
in evidence against you'

'Yeah? Well my Dad's more against
the teachers than your Dad'

'I'm not surprised it was a well-kept
secret. I'd never heard of either of
them'

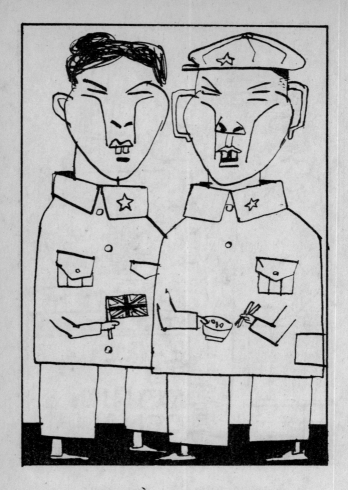

'Funny thing about British royalty.
See one, and three hours later you
want to see another'

'Judging from the Lower Fifth's response to extra prep, most of them already have an elementary grasp'

'And how long's the walk going to
be this time?'

'So, you're being released? Neither
am I'

'Verily, they fell off the back of a
lorry'

'Remind me, is that good or bad
news?'

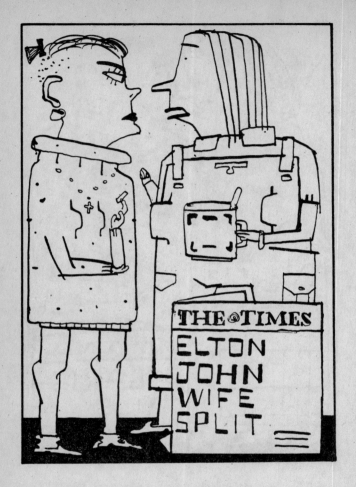

'I wonder who'll get custody of his
wardrobe?'

'Today we did Maths, French and
Intermediate Homosexuality'

'At least the kids won't have to be
given the day off'

'You realise she'll now hold office
into the 22nd Century'

'I had no idea he played rugby'

'I'm surprised that no one's blamed
us'

'On your own, dear? Why not play
"Gang of Four"?'

'How long before someone's charged
with insider dealing?'

'No, it doesn't remind me of the
Blitz. It reminds me of when I had
a job.'